This book belongs to:

_____

_____

_____

First published 2000 by Walker Books Ltd
87 Vauxhall Walk, London SE11 5HJ

This edition published 2011

2 4 6 8 10 9 7 5 3 1

© 2000 Lucy Cousins
Lucy Cousins font © 2000 Lucy Cousins

"Maisy" Audio Visual Series produced by King Rollo Films for
Universal Pictures International Visual Programming

Maisy™. Maisy is a registered trademark of Walker Books Ltd, London.

The moral right of the author/illustrator has been asserted

Printed in China

British Library Cataloguing in Publication Data:
a catalogue record for this book is available from the British Library

ISBN 978-1-4063-3476-0

www.walker.co.uk
www.maisyfun.co.uk

Maisy's Bus

Lucy Cousins

WALKER BOOKS
AND SUBSIDIARIES

LONDON · BOSTON · SYDNEY · AUCKLAND

Maisy is driving her bus today.

Who will be at bus stop number 1?

It's Cyril.

Hello, Cyril.

Little Black Cat is waiting at bus stop number 2.

Hello,
Little Black Cat.

Brmm, brmm!

Who will be at bus stop number 3?

It's Tallulah,
waiting in the rain.

Hello, Tallulah.

Eddie is waiting at bus stop number 4.

Will there be room on the bus?

Hooray! There's room for everyone.

Brmm, brmm! Where is Maisy going now?

Bus stop number 5.

It's time to get off, everyone.

Oops! Wake up,
Little Black Cat.

This is the last stop.

Bye bye, everyone.
Bye bye, Maisy.

Brmm, brmm!